THE
UNLUCKY LAUNCH

Don't Miss Any of Astrid's
Out-of-This-World Adventures!

The Astronomically Grand Plan

The Unlucky Launch

ASTRID THE ASTRONAUT

THE
UNLUCKY LAUNCH

By Rie Neal ★ Illustrated by Talitha Shipman

ALADDIN
New York London Toronto Sydney New Delhi

❦ ALADDIN • An imprint of Simon & Schuster Children's Publishing Division • 1230 Avenue of the Americas, New York, New York 10020 • First Aladdin paperback edition July 2022 • Text copyright © 2022 by Rie Neal • Illustrations copyright © 2022 by Talitha Shipman • Also available in an Aladdin hardcover edition. • All rights reserved, including the right of reproduction in whole or in part in any form. • ALADDIN and related logo are registered trademarks of Simon & Schuster, Inc. • For information about special discounts for bulk purchases, please contact Simon & Schuster Special Sales at 1-866-506-1949 or business@simonandschuster.com. • The Simon & Schuster Speakers Bureau can bring authors to your live event. For more information or to book an event contact the Simon & Schuster Speakers Bureau at 1-866-248-3049 or visit our website at www.simonspeakers.com. • Book designed by Laura Lyn DiSiena • The illustrations for this book were rendered digitally. • The text of this book was set in Ionic No 5. • Manufactured in the United States of America 0522 OFF • 2 4 6 8 10 9 7 5 3 1 • Library of Congress Cataloging-in-Publication Data | Names: Neal, Rie, author. | Shipman, Talitha, illustrator. | Title: The unlucky launch / by Rie Neal ; illustrated by Talitha Shipman. | Description: First Aladdin paperback edition. | New York : Aladdin, 2022. | Series: Astrid the astronaut ; book 2 | Audience: Ages 6 to 9. | Summary: When Astrid and her fellow Shooting Stars build a rocket, Astrid is hoping to impress guest helper, Lana, to score a tour of Space-E headquarters, but when she and her classmates discover Lana does not know much about rockets, Astrid is unsure if she should speak up. | Identifiers: LCCN 2021052732 (print) | LCCN 2021052733 (ebook) | ISBN 9781534481510 (hardcover) | ISBN 9781534481503 (paperback) | ISBN 9781534481527 (ebook) | Subjects: CYAC: Middle schools—Fiction. | Schools—Fiction. | Cooperativeness—Fiction. | Rockets (Aeronautics)—Fiction. | LCGFT: Fiction. | Classification: LCC PZ7.1.N3826 Un 2022 (print) | LCC PZ7.1.N3826 (ebook) | DDC [Fic] —dc23 | LC record available at https://lccn.loc.gov/2021052732 | LC ebook record available at https://lccn.loc.gov/2021052733

FOR JMAC & SL,
FOR BEING THE BEST KIDS
(AND ROCKET TESTERS) EVER
—R. N.

TO MICHAEL,
MY ROCKET-PROPELLED BESTIE
—T. S.

CONTENTS

★ CHAPTER 1 ★

THE SPACE-E LAUNCH

"T-minus five minutes," said the announcer.

My eyes were glued to the screen. Space-E's new rocket was about to launch. It was tall and white. Steam curled off the sides. Our whole class was watching.

Mr. Klein, my third-grade teacher, clapped his hands. "Isn't this exciting?"

"Nothing is happening," Hallie, my best

friend, whispered. She shaded parts of the sky she was drawing. Mr. Klein had let her finish it while we watched. Hallie always wanted more time on her art.

"They have to check lots of things before they can launch," I whispered back.

But I wanted the announcer to say more too. Mr. Klein had set the clip-on microphone for my hearing aids right in front of the speakers. I could hear it okay. They just weren't saying much.

The camera switched to show all of Space-E's employees. They were watching the launch too. They squeezed one another's hands. Some were crying.

"I bet the astronauts get tired of waiting," Hallie said. She added sparkle gel to her sky.

I pointed to her paper. "That looks nice."

"Thanks! I know the stars aren't really different colors like this."

"Some are. My mom says stars can be almost any color."

"Really?"

I nodded. The screen was back on the rocket. The announcer was still quiet, though. Waiting.

"What are you going to be for Costume Day next Thursday?" I asked Hallie. Our school had a few Spirit Days throughout the year—Twin Day, School Colors Day, Sports Day, and things like that. But my favorite one was coming up: Costume Day!

Hallie capped her pen. "I'm going to be Princess CATastrophe. From *AstroCat*. I have the cat ears and the cape."

"Oh, cool." I wished I had thought of something like that. Still, my costume was going to be amazing. "I'm going to be—"

"T-minus fifteen seconds," the announcer said.

I whirled to face the TV.

"Here we go!" said Mr. Klein.

"Ten . . . nine . . . eight . . ."

Our class counted with the announcer. Hallie and I joined in too.

"Three . . . two . . . one."

"Ignition," said the announcer. A jet of fire burst out from the bottom of the rocket. Smoke filled the screen. "Liftoff!" And the rocket shot up into the air.

The people who worked at Space-E cheered. They hugged and slapped one another on the back.

"Wow," I breathed.

Hallie grinned. "That was awesome!"

The class clapped, and Mr. Klein clicked off

the TV. "What did you guys think?"

I put my hand in the air, and Mr. Klein nodded. "Astrid?"

"I wish I could see a rocket take off in person!"

He smiled. "Maybe one day you will. Lots of people do. Even getting to go to Space-E would be amazing, I think. Most launches are in Florida, but Space-E headquarters is right here in the Bay Area. You have to be invited to get a tour, though."

Wow . . . get a tour of Space-E? They were one of the biggest space tech companies ever.

Mr. Klein said we were super close to them. But they felt as far away as Mars. How did people get invited to visit?

I didn't know, but I was going to make it my mission to find out.

★ CHAPTER 2 ★

THE BEST MENTOR EVER

I hefted my backpack up onto the lab table.

"Hey, Astrid." Veejay perched on the stool next to mine.

"Did you watch the launch today?" I asked.

Veejay shook his head. "I wish! We had a spelling test then."

"Ugh, I'm sorry you missed it."

Kids filed into the STEM lab. It was after

school, and time for Shooting Stars, the space-themed club I was a part of. Ms. Ruiz, the teacher who ran the club, held out her hand next to me. I gave her the clip-on mic for my hearing aids, and she put it on her shirt. Today, her nails were apple green.

"Did you watch the launch?" I asked.

Her eyes sparkled. "I wouldn't miss it!" Her voice now boomed through my hearing aids. "I'm a big fan of Space-E." She nodded to some people standing by her desk. "In fact, Lana—in the red shirt—she works there as an intern. She's writing some of the code for their next mission."

My eyes bugged. "Really?"

Ms. Ruiz nodded and went back to her desk.

The young woman she'd pointed to had freckles, like me, but her skin was darker.

Her hair was pulled back in a messy bun, and she had a ball cap on with Space-E's logo on it. A pencil and a pen stuck out of her bun at odd angles.

But why was she *here*? And the others, too?

I turned to Veejay. "That woman over there works for Space-E!"

Veejay shrugged. "Cool."

He was way too calm. "Have *you* ever met anybody who works there?"

"No, I don't think so."

Ms. Ruiz clapped her hands to get our attention. "We're going to start a special Astro Mission today," she said. "In honor of Space-E's launch, we're going to build our own rockets!"

I gaped at Veejay. He grinned back.

"First, you'll get into groups of four. Each group will get a box." Ms. Ruiz pointed to a stack behind her. "You can *only* use the items in the box. And water, if you need it." She pointed to some jugs by the door. "We'll launch next Friday. The rocket that flies the highest will earn three points on the Astro Board for their team members. And to celebrate we'll have a party after the launches!"

I glanced at the giant grid behind Ms. Ruiz's desk. The person with the most points at the end of the year would get a scholarship to Space Camp. We'd had six Astro Missions so far this year. Veejay and I had a lot of points, but we weren't in the lead. Pearl was. Across the room she adjusted her flight jacket. She looked very proud of herself.

"And I'd like you to meet my friends here," Ms. Ruiz said. "Staci, Ming, Ayesha, Trent, and Lana. They're all college students and are helping us out *for free,* so be nice to them!" We giggled. "Once you have a team, grab one of them to work with you. Go!"

Stools scraped against the floor. Chatter filled the room.

Ella and Dominic ran up.

"Hey, you guys want to be a team?" Ella panted.

"Yes! Let's get Lana!" I glanced at Veejay, and he nodded.

"Who?" asked Dominic.

I pointed. "She works for Space-E. She'll know a ton about rockets!"

"Great!" said Ella.

We hurried up to the front. Ms. Ruiz handed Ella one of the large boxes.

Lana stood with the other mentors. She was scrolling on her phone now.

I stepped up in front of her. "Hi."

She jumped, almost dropping her phone.

"Will you work with us?" I asked.

"Oh! Sure." She hurried to tuck the phone into her pocket. "Did you guys get a box?"

"Yep. I'm Astrid, by the way." I led her to our lab table. Ella and Dominic had pulled up stools to join us.

This was going great. Lana was going to help us build the best rocket.

And . . . what if you just had to know somebody at Space-E to get a tour? Now we knew Lana. Maybe she would take us there! I imagined the doors to Space-E opening wide. *It's Astrid Peterson,* someone would say. *She's a friend of Lana's. She was* invited *here.*

"Hey, crew. I'm Lana." She gave a wave to

the others. "Well, let's . . . uh . . . look in the box, I guess."

We all peered inside. There were *lots* of things in the box.

"Do we have to use everything?" Dominic asked as he pulled out a rubbery tube.

"No, no," said Lana. "We just need to build a rocket." She had her phone out again. Biting her lip, she looked between it and the box.

I peeked over her shoulder. She was looking at rocket plans for us!

"What kind should we build?" Ella took out a big, empty soda bottle. "My mom and I built a water rocket last year. It was for my science fair project. They go really high."

"Great!" said Veejay. He and Ella picked through the box.

Lana was still scrolling on her phone.

I cleared my throat. "So . . . you work for Space-E, right?"

She squinted at the screen. "I sure do!"

I thought back to the rocket we'd watched today in class.

"Did you get to watch the launch there?"

She nodded.

"What was it like?"

Her eyes glowed. "Epic."

"I bet it was." I sighed, imagining what it would be like to watch it with all the people cheering. "So . . . do you ever get to bring people to Space-E for tours?"

Lana frowned at her phone. Maybe she didn't hear me.

Dominic wrapped the tube around his neck like a scarf. "How do I look?" he said in a funny voice.

Ella giggled.

"Pearl's team is already building," Veejay said. "We need to hurry up!"

"Don't worry. I'm finding us the *fastest* plans," Lana said. "Aha! *This* one." She showed us some rocket plans on her phone.

Ella frowned. "That doesn't look right. I know how to make a water rocket. I can show you guys." She turned the bottle upside down. She moved it up, making blast-off noises.

"Look, I can't stay long today," said Lana. "I have to get back to Space-E. But I promise, this rocket will be really fast to build." Lana shook her phone as she plucked the bottle out of Ella's hands. "*We* are going to build the best rocket of all. And we won't have to get wet."

I grinned. "Yeah!"

Lana nodded to me. "Astrid, right?"

She remembered my name! Space-E felt closer already.

"Wait—we're not using water?" Ella asked.

"Nope! We're going to use *air* as a propellant. This little baby will shoot our rocket into the sky when we step on it." She squeezed the empty bottle. *Crunch*. Then she let the sides pop back into place. Another crunch.

Dominic laughed. "You mean like a stomp rocket? The ones little kids play with?"

"Yes," said Lana. "But a . . . uh . . ." She glanced again at her phone. "A better one than those. Hand me that tube."

Dominic took the rubber tube off his neck. "Hey, there's a hole in it!"

Lana examined it. "He's right. I'll just go swap it. Be right back."

As soon as she'd left, Ella leaned in. "I don't

think Lana knows much about rockets."

"Of course she does," I whispered back. "She works for Space-E!"

"Technically, that doesn't mean she's ever built a rocket," Veejay said.

"But she probably has," I said. Across the room Pearl's mentor laughed at a joke she'd made. Their group wasn't making a stomp rocket. They were putting fins on the soda bottle. They were making a water rocket.

I squeezed our bottle. *Crunch, crunch.* Would an air rocket really be better?

Yes, of course it would. Ms. Ruiz always said there was more than one solution. And Lana had experience. Besides, if we were nice to her, maybe she would take us on that tour.

I took a deep breath. "We should trust Lana. Just because she has a different idea for a rocket doesn't mean it's wrong. She works for *Space-E.*"

My friends just shrugged.

Ella folded her arms. "Fine."

I smiled, sitting up straight. We were on track for winning the Astro Mission. *And* for going to Space-E.

★ CHAPTER 3 ★

THE PING-PONG HELMET

"Have you done your homework?" My big sister, Stella, stared me down with her best Mom face.

"Be good, you guys. I'm off to work." Dad kissed our heads, then closed himself into his office.

I started for the living room, but Stella blocked my way.

"I want to check the printer!" I tossed my backpack onto the floor and ducked past her.

"Astrid!" She stomped her foot. "I'm in charge, remember?"

Ever since she'd started middle school, Stella thought she was big stuff. Now Mom and Dad had made it worse. They'd put her in charge of me after school. Dad was home grading papers, so he'd be there if we really needed him. Otherwise, Stella was in charge. Way too much power for an eleven-year-old, if you asked me.

I crossed our living room in three big leaps.

The 3D printer sat on top of a low cabinet, humming away. Spools of plastic were stacked next to it. The printer head moved back and forth, melting the plastic to make something new. Today, it was the helmet for my Costume

Day outfit. I'd wanted to be an astronaut for *forever*. I finally had a flight suit—a friend of Mom's gave it to us as a hand-me-down. But they'd lost the helmet. And the costume *had* to have a helmet.

"It's almost done!" I squealed. "The last piece of my costume!" I turned back to Stella. "What can we have for a snack?"

Stella folded her arms. "Apple slices. And ... *half* a cookie."

"Half?!" I frowned. "Dad lets me have a whole one."

Stella sighed. "Fine. But with milk."

"Deal." I raced into the kitchen. Dad had made kitchen sink cookies. He called them that because of the saying "everything but the kitchen sink," which meant anything and everything. Today, the cookies had coconut, caramel, and peanuts in them. But they changed every time he made them.

"Do you think Dad likes teaching the new class?" I asked Stella. I bit into my cookie. Ooey gooey caramel melted in my mouth.

Dad was a high school history teacher, but he'd just started teaching an extra class—3D printing. The school had let Dad borrow a printer to keep at home. He was learning at the same time as his students. It was weird to think of Dad not knowing something.

Stella set two cups of milk on the table. "I think he likes the *printing* part."

I giggled. We both eyed the 3D printer again. A basket of printed things sat next to it—some of them finished, and some of them failed. He'd been printing a *lot*.

A beep sounded, and the printer head stopped.

"It's done!" I bolted down the hall to Dad's office.

"Astrid!" Stella ran after me. "Dad is working. This is *not* an emergency!"

"But we can't touch the printer without him!"

Before I could knock, though, the door burst open. Dad grinned. "Is it finished?"

I nodded, and he zoomed past me. Stella and I ran to catch up.

Dad held the helmet up, grinning. "It's beautiful!"

But Stella wrinkled her nose. "Is it supposed to look like that?"

It *sort of* looked like an astronaut helmet. But really, it looked more like a huge, flattened

Ping-Pong ball. The sides were way too thin.

"Looks just like my design," Dad said. His chest puffed up.

Dad had designed it himself? "Um . . . yeah," I said. "It's great, Dad."

There were lots of free designs online. Writing your own was really hard. And sure, Dad had to learn on *something* . . . but I sort of wished it hadn't been my helmet.

"Let's try it on." He slid the helmet down onto my head. My hearing aids squeaked in protest. The sides of the helmet squished my cheeks, and it wouldn't go down all the way. "Well, it's not perfect, but it's not bad. Here, look in a mirror." Dad walked me into the hall.

Well . . . I did look a *little* like an astronaut.

"Hmm." Dad shook his head. "I think I got

the size wrong. Too bad I used up all the white filament."

Stella shrugged. "You could be something else."

"No, it's fine," I said quickly. "I *have* to be an astronaut."

"I have a bunch of extra red." Dad shrugged. "I could try again."

But what if the next helmet was even worse? Besides, I'd never seen a *red* astronaut helmet.

"That's okay, Dad."

"All right, suit yourself. Well, back to work." Dad closed himself into the office again.

Stella pulled the helmet off my head. My hair stuck up all over. "Why didn't you ask him to try again? Plenty of his prints have failed. He's still learning this stuff. If the helmet doesn't fit right, he needs to know."

I smoothed down my hair. "I couldn't. You heard him. It was the first one he did himself. It's fine. I like it." I grabbed the helmet back. "I'm sure real helmets aren't that comfortable, either."

⋆ CHAPTER 4 ⋆

LANA'S—I MEAN, OUR—ROCKET

On Friday I skipped into Shooting Stars. "Hi, Veejay."

"Hey, Astrid. I got the box. Ready to build a rocket?"

"Absolutely!"

Dominic joined us. "Woo-hoo! Rocket time!"

Ella sat on a stool across from us. "I still think water would be better," she grumbled.

Lana's bag slapped down on the table, making me jump. She was out of breath, like she'd been running to get here.

"Will the air rocket go really high?" Dominic asked her.

"A hundred feet!" Lana grinned.

I had no idea what a hundred feet looked like. But it sure sounded like a lot!

She dug through her bag, then pulled out some papers. "Here. I made this printed copy for you guys."

Dominic leaned over the plans. "That looks pretty good."

"Great," Veejay said. "We just need to be ready to practice by Monday."

I imagined our rocket shooting into the clouds. Lana would be clapping for us. Maybe she'd even take us on a tour next weekend,

after the launch. But first, I'd have to ask her—
again. Because maybe she hadn't heard me
the first time.

"Earth to Astrid." Veejay elbowed me.

They were all staring at me. I hadn't been paying attention.

"Can you get out the cork, please?" Lana asked me. "That'll be the nose of the rocket."

"Oh. Right." Cheeks warm, I fished around and pulled it out.

"And a sheet of paper." Lana nodded at Veejay.

He grabbed paper from the box.

"And the plastic pipe. That'll be our launch tube."

"I got it," Dominic said.

Lana squinted at the plans. "Okay . . . now we roll the paper around the launch tube. That'll make it just the right size. We tape it so it stays, and then slide it off the tube."

Dominic started rolling. Ella got the tape ready.

I cleared my throat. "So," I said to Lana. "What's it like to work for Space-E? Do you get to watch *all* the launches?"

Lana grinned. "I mean, just on the monitors, but yeah. They broadcast it in the lobby. We all stop what we're doing to watch. I was so caught up in my code this week, I almost missed it."

"Wow," I breathed.

"What do we do next?" Ella asked.

Lana bent over the paper again. "Uh . . . right. Make sure the cork is taped inside one end of the paper tube."

I took a deep breath. "D-do you ever give tours to people?" I asked it nice and loud this time.

But Lana's phone buzzed right then. She took it out of her pocket and frowned. "What?"

she said to me. "Oh . . . uh, I guess. I took my mom to visit once."

I beamed at Veejay. He gave me a thumbs-up.

"Okay, done!" Dominic said.

Lana tucked her phone away and slipped the rocket off the tube. It just looked like a roll of paper with a cork at one end. And . . . well . . . it was.

"Will that really fly a hundred feet?" Dominic asked.

"Aren't we going to add fins?" Ella said. "You have to have fins so it will fly straight."

Lana nodded. "I was just going to say that."

Next to me, Ella hmphed.

I shot Ella a look that I hoped said, *She knows what she's doing.*

Veejay cut out three triangles. I held them in place, and he taped them to the sides.

"Looks great," Lana said. "Now we build the launcher." She ran her finger over the plans.

I swallowed. "So . . . do you think you could take *us* on a tour of Space-E?"

But Lana's phone went off again then. She groaned as she pulled it out. "Uh . . . maybe?" she said to me.

The bell rang. We started cleaning up.

"I have to dash," said Lana. "Good work, crew. See you Monday!"

We waved, but Lana was already out the door.

"She said maybe!" I whispered to Veejay.

But Ella leaned over. "*Maybe* isn't *yes*." She tossed her braids over her shoulders and stomped out.

"What's with her?" asked Veejay.

"I don't know," I said. But I did know. I just thought we should listen to Lana.

I hoped Ella would think so, too, when our rocket won.

★ CHAPTER 5 ★

THE POOPTASTIC LAUNCH

On Monday we were the first group to finish our rocket. But we had to do it without Lana.

We followed the plans she'd left us. One end of the rubber hose went around the launch tube. The other fit around the empty soda bottle.

"So, to launch it, we just stomp on the bottle?" Dominic asked.

I shrugged. "I guess."

"Where's Lana?" Ella whined. "She's supposed to be our mentor."

The rocket sure didn't look like it could fly a hundred feet. But if it did, we'd probably win the Astro Mission. And Lana would be happy.

"Ms. Ruiz said she's working on Space-E's next mission. She's an important person," I said.

Lana finally walked in, fifteen minutes late.

Ella frowned. "Where were you?"

Lana set her bag down. "Sorry, guys."

"We finished!" Dominic held up the rocket. "I wore my lucky socks today. For the test launch. Can we try it out now?"

As we headed out to the field, the other groups were still building. Veejay grinned. "Maybe Lana was right," he said. "It *was* really fast to build an air rocket."

"Plus, we don't have to carry any water," Dominic said.

But Ella chewed her lip. "Ms. Ruiz got so much water ready. Are you guys sure we weren't supposed to build a *water* rocket?"

Lana lagged behind us, scowling at her phone.

I put my hands on my hips. "It's *Ms. Ruiz*. More than one solution, right?"

Kids in after-school care bounced balls and played tag. At the end of the last building, Hallie waved.

"Hey, Hallie!" I said, running over. "What are you doing?"

There were pencil lines all over the wall. A drop cloth covered the ground. Hallie and the other kids wore giant smocks.

"Petite Picassos is painting a mural!"

she said. "We get to put *art* on a *building*. Amazing, right?"

"Wow," I said. "I can't wait to see it!"

"What are you guys doing?" Hallie asked.

"Astrid, come on!" shouted Veejay. They'd gotten ahead of me.

"Testing our rocket," I told Hallie. "Gotta go!"

I ran to catch up just as our team reached the field.

"Watch out for dog poop!" Dominic called. There were signs up saying you couldn't bring dogs here, but people did it anyway.

Lana froze, one leg in the air. "What?"

"It's fine. Just keep your eyes open," Veejay said.

"This spot looks good," Ella said. We stopped and waited for Lana. She was texting someone on her phone as she picked her way through the grass.

Dominic set down the box with our rocket in it.

As he and Ella set it up, I scooted over to Lana. "So . . . about the tour. Do you think we could go next weekend?"

But Lana made a face. "I don't know, Astrid. I'll have to wait and see how *this* goes." On the word "this," she waggled her phone.

What did that mean?

She'd been looking up rocket plans on her

phone. So . . . did "this" mean our launch? Like, if our rocket flopped, she wouldn't take us?

Way back by the STEM lab, more kids were coming out. Another group was about to test.

"We have to hurry," I told Lana.

"Yeah, we don't want anyone to steal our idea," Veejay said.

"You mean Lana's idea," muttered Ella.

I squatted down to hold the rocket in place.

"Can I jump on it?" asked Dominic.

"Go for it!" Lana tucked her phone into her back pocket.

"Wait . . . how will we know how high it goes?" asked Ella.

"Oh no." Lana looked back to the lab and groaned. "We were supposed to pick up an altimeter."

"A what?" I asked.

"It's a little device you tape to the rocket," said Lana. "To measure how high it goes."

That seemed pretty important. "Can one of us go back and get it?" I asked.

"We don't have time!" Veejay pointed. The other group was now crossing the blacktop. "Let's just do a test flight before they get here."

"Veejay's right," Lana said.

So Dominic jumped into the air. He landed on the bottle with a crunch.

The rocket shot into the sky!

I craned my neck back to watch. It got super tiny. Then it flipped, zooming back down to crash-land in the grass.

"Whoa," breathed Veejay.

"That was awesome!" Dominic cheered. "It went so high!"

I stuck my chin out at Ella. "See? I told you

Lana knew what to do." But Ella just frowned.

Lana was on her phone again. "Great job, guys!"

Had she not been watching?

"Yeah, I'm here," Lana said. But now her phone was at her ear. I couldn't make it all out, but she said something about "code" and "in an hour."

Ella glared at me. Like it was my fault Lana was always working.

"What?" I hissed to her. "She's on a work call. Like I said, *important person*." I realized then that when Lana had shaken her phone at me, she meant *work*. Of course. She had to wait and see how work was going before she could say yes to a tour. It made me feel both better and worse at the same time. I wished she could pay more attention to us.

"Is this yours, Astrid?" Pearl called. Her group had reached the field. She pointed at a clump in the grass, a smirk on her face. Behind her, her group was setting up their rocket. Their mentor didn't have her phone out. She was high-fiving them and smiling.

We stomped over to where Pearl stood.

It was our rocket, all right—in a St. Bernard–sized pile of dog poop.

"Ewww!" we groaned.

Pearl bent over, laughing. "I guess we know who *won't* be winning this Astro Mission."

She ran to join her group. Lana was still back by our launch site, talking into her phone.

Dominic frowned at the poop-covered rocket. "I guess these socks *aren't* lucky. What a pooptastic day!"

I balled my hands into fists. "We have to

build a new rocket. We have to win!"

"Agreed." Ella nodded.

Veejay folded his arms. "We're way behind the other groups now."

And then Pearl's group's rocket launched. A jet of water snaked out of the bottle, pushing it up. It flew higher and higher.

"Did their rocket just disappear?" asked Dominic.

I gulped. "Yep."

We watched as it sailed back down, nose-first, and landed in the grass at our feet, but *not* in the dog poop. Pearl's team cheered. Their mentor gave them high fives. She looked just as thrilled as they were.

Lana joined us, finally off her phone. "Huh," she said. "But don't worry, guys. We've got them beat."

She thought ours had gone higher?

I glanced nervously at Veejay. He raised an eyebrow back.

Pearl ran over to pick up her group's rocket. She peered at a tiny device taped to the side. "Ninety-three feet!" she shouted in our faces. Her group cheered as she ran back to them.

But Lana just grinned. "See? The website said ours would go a *hundred* feet. You guys rock. Let's clean up and head back."

Lana's phone buzzed—*again*. "I'll meet you guys back at the lab," she said as she answered it.

As we followed Lana back, Ella motioned for us to slow down. So Lana couldn't hear.

"I don't think our rocket went a hundred feet," she said.

Hallie bounced over to us from her painting. When she saw our faces, she frowned. "What's wrong?"

"Could you see from here?" I swallowed. "Whose rocket went higher? Ours or the other group's?"

"Oh, the other group's, for sure. It went, like, twice as high. But yours was great too. Is . . . is it a competition?"

I slapped my forehead.

Dominic pinched the poopy rocket by its only clean fin. He plugged his nose with his other hand. "The website said *up to* one hundred feet. That doesn't mean it *will* go that high."

Ella folded her arms. "I think we should build a water rocket."

"Me too," Dominic said. Veejay nodded.

I swallowed. After seeing the other group's,

I wanted to build a rocket like that, too.

"We have to speak up." Ella put her hands on hips. "Astrid, you should tell Lana."

They all turned to me, waiting.

"What?!" I said. "Why me?"

"Lana likes you the best," said Ella. "Because you were all gushy about Space-E."

"I wasn't *gushy*."

"Yeah, you were." Veejay shifted the box. "That's not a bad thing. It just means maybe she'll listen to you."

Another group passed us on their way out to the field. A girl saw our poopy rocket and backed away.

"So . . . will you do it?" Ella asked.

They stared me down.

"Uh . . . sure."

"Good. I'm dumping this." Dominic held the

rocket over a trash can. "Goodbye, first rocket. You lived a good life." And Lana's poopy rocket disappeared into the garbage.

★ CHAPTER 6 ★

CHICKENING OUT

The STEM lab was almost empty when we got back. Most groups were out testing their rockets.

Lana waited at our table. "There you guys are! Did you get lost?"

Veejay plopped the box onto the table.

"The rocket was covered in dog poop," Dominic said. "We threw it away."

Lana frowned. "Oh." Her eyes darted between her phone and the box. "Oh no. Well ... I guess we need to build another one, then."

She did not look happy about it.

Ella raised her eyebrows at me.

I stared at the floor.

Lana picked through the box. "We'll need another cork. Looks like our soda bottle cracked, too. Better get a whole new box."

"She's going to have us make the same kind," Dominic hissed. "Tell her now."

"Astrid has something to say first," Ella told Lana.

But would she still take us to Space-E if we told her we didn't like her idea? It wasn't fair. Why did *I* have to be the one to tell her? My hands started to sweat.

"Astrid?" Lana prompted. "What's up?"

My throat went dry.

"I . . . I mean, we . . ." I swallowed. "We just wanted to say . . ."

Lana's forehead crinkled. I knew she didn't have tons of free time. In my head I saw the doors to Space-E closing. There would be no one there to let me in. No tour. Nothing.

"We think . . . you're doing a great job," I blurted.

Dominic groaned. Ella narrowed her eyes at me.

But Lana's face relaxed. "Whew!" she said. "I was afraid you were going to say something else."

"Yeah . . . like the truth," Ella muttered.

"I'll get us a new box," I said, jumping up before any of them could argue.

"Thanks, Astrid." Lana winked. "I knew you were a keeper."

She called me a *keeper*. My heart got big like a balloon.

Then Ella's glare popped it.

I hurried up to the front of the room, where Ms. Ruiz sat at her desk.

"Astrid, hi. What's up?"

"We . . . um . . . we need a new box," I said.

"Great job!" She bounced out of her chair and over to some shelves. She set a brand-new box in front of me.

I frowned. "Why do you say that?"

"Because it means you're trying new things, to see what works best. Not what you *want* to work best. Or what *someone else* wants to work best. If you only listen to what you want to hear, that's called bias. Bias has no place in science."

"Bias." I repeated the new word. It tasted like a sour lemon lollipop. We *weren't* doing

what worked best. We were doing what Lana wanted to do—whatever was fastest. And I was backing her up.

Ms. Ruiz winked at me. "Never be afraid to stand up for science, Astrid."

"Thanks," I mumbled. I hoisted the box up and shuffled back to our table.

Stand up for science, she'd said. But a tour of Space-E would be the best science ever. So, standing up for science meant keeping Lana happy. And making sure the rocket was fast to build. Right?

But as I sat down at the table, my friends wouldn't look at me. I knew why they were mad. I was mad at me too, for not being able to decide. Which "science" should I be standing up for—Space-E or the Astro Mission?

★ CHAPTER 7 ★
CRAAACK!

"What's with you?" Stella poked me.

I picked at my kitchen sink cookie. She took a big, chewy bite of hers. "Mmm . . . this batch has chocolate chips."

I sighed. "We're not going to win the Astro Mission." *And Lana may not take us to Space-E,* I added in my head. Double bad luck.

"When is it?" asked Stella.

"Friday. But our mentor is always working. She didn't even watch our test launch."

Stella tapped her chin, thinking. "You need cheering up. Want to try on your costume?"

I shrugged. "Sure."

Five minutes later we stood in front of the hallway mirror.

The astronaut outfit was perfect. I just wished my helmet looked that good. I pulled it down over my head carefully. My hearing aids squeaked again. My puffy curls pushed back against the too-thin sides of the helmet. But I wanted it on all the way this time. So I pushed harder.

CRACK.

I froze. "Uh . . ."

Stella slid the helmet off my head and

handed it to me. There
was a giant crack run-
ning across the whole
back of it.

"No!" I moaned. "I
can't wear it like this."

"I'm sorry, Astrid,"
Stella said. "Why didn't
you tell Dad it was too
small?"

"Because I *wanted* it to work," I whispered.

Dad's office door opened. I hid the helmet
behind my back, but I wasn't fast enough. His
face fell.

"Dad, I'm sorry. It just—"

"It broke, didn't it?" Dad scratched his
chin. "I thought it might. I'm sorry, Astro Girl. I

could print you another one. When is Costume Day again?"

"Thursday," I sighed. The day before the rocket launch.

Nothing was working. Not my costume, not the rocket . . .

Wait. This was just like the rocket. I knew there were problems with the helmet. But I wanted it to work, so I said it was fine. I knew the air rocket wasn't the best idea, too. But I wanted Lana to be happy. So I didn't stick up for Ella, and now we were going to lose the Astro Mission.

Ms. Ruiz had said to "stand up for science." Science meant listening to other ideas. Not just the ones we *wanted* to work. And maybe it wasn't too late—for the rocket *or* for my costume.

"It's okay, Dad. Really." I gave him a hug. "I have an idea. Do you think you could print me something else instead?"

"Well, sure, kiddo. Like what?"

"I'll tell you all about it. But first I have to make a phone call!" I handed him the helmet and sprinted to the kitchen.

★ CHAPTER 8 ★

STANDING UP FOR SCIENCE—AND ELLA

It took half the week to find a time we were all free. Dominic was seeing his grandparents that night. Veejay had math club the next day after school. Ella had to go to the dentist on Wednesday.

So Thursday—Costume Day—I waited for my friends after school on the blacktop. Maybe my costume would bring me luck. I'd need it.

Hallie had come with me to wait. She shook her shimmery cape. Her cat ears had a tiara attached.

"That's *definitely* Princess CATastrophe," I told her for the millionth time. "I love it."

Other kids ran past us with funny hats, face paint, and masks on.

She grinned. "And you're AstroCat! We go together. Where did you get the headband?"

I fingered the plastic cat-ear headband. "My dad 3D printed it," I said. "I wouldn't have gotten the idea if you hadn't told me about your costume."

Veejay walked up in a top hat and a wide, silly tie. We weren't in the same class, so it was the first time we'd seen each other's costumes. "Hey!" he said, pointing at me. "AstroCat!"

I squinted back at him. "Who are you?"

He pointed to the hat. "I'm Gusto the Grand. You know, from the graphic novels? He's a magician."

Dominic skipped up then, wearing a super-hero cape. Ella, wearing a box painted to look like a robot, was right behind him.

"Thanks for coming," I told my friends.

"I've got to go," said Hallie. "See you tomorrow. And good luck," she whispered to me.

As Hallie skipped to the front of the school, I turned back to my other friends.

Ella tried to cross her arms, but they bumped into the box. She huffed instead. "So . . . you really think we should build a water rocket? Now? The launch is *tomorrow*, Astrid."

I took a deep breath. "Yes. I know."

Veejay frowned. "What about Lana?"

I shrugged. "I don't know yet. But we can tell her tomorrow. I think we should do it Ella's way. If you guys still want to."

Dominic gave a thumbs-up. "I'm in."

Veejay bit his lip. "But Ms. Ruiz said we could only use what was in the box."

"I already checked one out." I toed the big box on the ground in front of us. "Ms. Ruiz said we could work out here, and she'd keep an eye on us from the lab."

"We won't have time to test it," Ella said.

"Right." I shrugged. "But you've done this before. You said the water rocket you built went really high, right?"

"Well . . . yeah. It did."

I nodded. "I think . . . maybe Lana was just trying to build a rocket fast. I'm sorry I didn't stick up for you. I just really wanted to see

Space-E. I thought if we did what she wanted, she would take us."

Ella took a deep breath. The robot box moved up and down with her shoulders. "We shouldn't have put it all on you," she said. "And maybe she'll still take us. Or maybe we can find another way to get a tour."

"Maybe," I said. But I said it to be nice. I was pretty sure Lana didn't have time. And how else would we get a tour? But . . . it was okay. I was standing up for science—and my friends.

Veejay reached into the box. He pulled out the empty soda bottle. "Let's get started."

Dominic tossed the tennis ball from the box up in the air. His arm got tangled in his cape. He caught the ball again, but just barely.

"We need that for the nose!" Ella grabbed it. "Be careful!"

And we dug through the box, letting Ella tell us what to do.

I wasn't sure what Lana would think about our new plan. Would she feel bad that we did it without her? I guessed I'd worry about that tomorrow. Today, we had a rocket to build.

CHAPTER 9

LAUNCH DAY

"Welcome to launch day!" Ms. Ruiz clipped my mic to her flight suit. She always wore her flight suit on Astro Mission days. Seeing it made me sit up straighter.

The entire lab cheered. Our mentors clapped too.

"I can't wait for the launch," Ella said.

"I can't wait for the *party*!" said Dominic.

It was Friday after school. Kids and mentors were busy getting their rockets ready for launch. But Lana wasn't there yet.

Maybe she wouldn't come today. Maybe we wouldn't have to talk to her at all.

And then she ran in, out of breath. "Sorry," she mouthed to Ms. Ruiz.

So much for that. Forget butterflies—my stomach was full of *mosquitoes*.

"I'll give everybody ten minutes. Then we'll meet out on the field." Ms. Ruiz began waving kids outside.

Lana rubbed her hands together. "You guys ready for liftoff?"

My throat was dry. "Um, Lana?"

Veejay stood next to me and nodded for me to keep going.

I swallowed. "We . . . we built a new

rocket," I said. It came out really soft.

Lana frowned, like she hadn't heard me.

Dominic pointed to the bag in Veejay's hand. "We ... uh ... This ..."

"We built a water rocket," I said, louder this time.

Lana blinked. "When did you do that?"

"Yesterday," Veejay said. "Ella told us what to do."

The other groups had all left the lab. Ms. Ruiz stood by the door, hand on the light switch. "Are you guys coming?"

"Yes," Ella called back.

"Oh," Lana said to us. Her cheeks got pink. "Well ... okay."

We filed out the door. Ella grabbed an altimeter from the basket by the door. After a pause, Lana followed.

"She's definitely upset," I whispered to Veejay.

"I mean, I feel bad, but I also want to have the best rocket," he said back. "Lana wasn't listening to us."

I bit my lip. Lana had listened to *me*. And I had convinced my friends that we shouldn't speak up.

There had to be a way I could fix this.

☆　☆　☆

"Okay, we're going to go down the line," Ms. Ruiz called. She was yelling so all the kids could hear her. Thanks to the clip-on mic, though, she was *really* loud for me.

The sun was bright out on the field. It was a perfect day for a launch.

Each group had set up their rocket. All of them were water rockets, but each one was different. One had a tennis ball for a nose, like ours. One had six fins. One had a weird skirt thing. I crossed my fingers, hoping ours would go the highest.

Lana stood behind us, hands in her pockets. For once she wasn't on her phone.

Ms. Ruiz nodded to the first group. They started pumping their bike pump up and down. It only took about ten seconds, and then—*WHOOSH!* The rocket sailed straight up.

"Wow," I breathed.

"Whoa," said Veejay.

Lana's mouth dropped open.

A kid ran to get the rocket. He called out a number. I could hear Ms. Ruiz out here, thanks to the mic. But not other kids that were far away.

I poked Ella. "What did he say?"

"A hundred twenty feet."

Gulp.

Ella swallowed. "Did you wear your lucky socks?" she asked Dominic.

"Nuh-uh," he said. "They didn't work before."

From the group next to us, Pearl put her nose in the air. "Ours is going to go higher than that. We tested it. Again."

"Ours is going to do great too." Lana stepped closer to us. "We have an expert." She pointed to Ella, who blushed.

I grinned up at Lana. She nodded back to me. Maybe things would be okay after all.

We watched the next two rockets—eighty-seven feet, then one hundred thirteen.

It was Pearl's group's turn. She pumped their bike pump up and down. *WHOOSH!* The

 76

rocket sailed up, but it made an arc instead of going straight up.

"No!" they wailed.

"It flew fine last time!" Pearl whined.

"They had a bent fin," Ella said. "I saw before they launched. That's why it didn't fly straight."

A kid came running back with the rocket. He said the number loud enough for me to hear. "Thirty-seven feet."

"Okay, last group!" Ms. Ruiz's voice was so loud in my hearing aids, it made me jump.

"That's us!" said Dominic.

I swallowed. We'd never tested our new rocket. At least we knew it wasn't broken from a crash-landing, but ... would it fly?

Veejay pointed across the blacktop. Hallie was jumping and waving. She was cheering us

on! I waved back, sort of glad she was too far away to see me sweating.

Ella chewed her lip.

"I'm glad we made the water rocket," I told her. "Even if we don't win. It was fun."

She smiled back. "Thanks, Astrid."

Dominic threw his weight into pumping. His glasses bounced on his nose. Air bubbled through the water. Finally, the cork popped out. The rocket shot upward, spraying us with water. It got smaller and smaller—until all we could see was sky.

★ CHAPTER 10 ★

A LUCKY SURPRISE

"Where did it go?" I asked.

Veejay shaded his eyes. Dominic's jaw dropped. Ella laughed.

And then the rocket was a tiny speck again. It got bigger—and faster.

"Look out!" I yelled. We ran for cover. The rocket bounced in the grass next to us.

Veejay picked it up. "No dog poop!" He ran

back, holding the rocket so we could all see the altimeter.

My jaw dropped.

Ella squealed, jumping up and down.

Lana peeked at it. "Wild."

Ms. Ruiz joined us. "May I?"

Veejay handed the rocket over. Ms. Ruiz tapped me on the shoulder. "Looks like someone stood up for science."

I grinned back. "Ella had a lot of good ideas. We just needed to listen to her."

"Listening to what *has* and *has not* worked in the past is part of science." Ms. Ruiz winked, then faced the rest of the kids. This time, I popped the earmolds out of my ears a little. Her voice was still plenty loud. "We have a winner!" she shouted. "Two hundred and five feet!"

"We did it!" I cheered.

Dominic pointed to his feet. "And I have *new lucky socks*!"

Veejay and I high-fived. Dominic whooped. Ella bounced up and down, grinning ear to ear.

We'd won the Astro Mission!

☆　☆　☆

On our way back to the lab, we skipped and laughed. We'd won, and now we were having a party for the rest of club time. But I still had one thing left to fix.

Hanging back, I let Lana catch up with me.

"I'm sorry we didn't tell you what we wanted sooner."

"No, *I'm* sorry." She shook her head. "I should've told Ms. Ruiz I couldn't help out. I've been super busy with this new project at work. And I'm taking classes this semester too. I've never actually launched a model rocket, either—can you believe it?"

After this Astro Mission, yes, I could believe it. But I didn't want to make Lana feel bad.

"It's okay," I said instead.

"But you know what? I was really impressed with you kids. You four really worked together as a team. That's important. It won't be long until *you* are ready to work for Space-E."

My face lit up. "You think so?"

"I know so. I won't be able to give you guys that tour you wanted, but . . . I did call in a favor from another intern." She jerked her head toward the lab.

"What is it?" I asked.

"It's not much. But you'll see." She slipped inside.

Hallie was waiting at the door. "You guys

83 ★
★★

did great. Those rockets were so cool!"

"Thanks!" I stopped to admire the mural as kids were cleaning up. They had painted tons of hands, in different skin tones. They were in a circle, all reaching toward the center.

"What do you think?" asked Hallie.

"Nice!" I tapped my chin. "It looks like . . . teamwork!"

She beamed. "Yeah! That's what it's supposed to be."

Veejay grabbed my arm. "Come on, Astrid! You're going to miss the party."

I waved to Hallie and ducked inside.

The lab was filled with excited kids. My friends waved us over to our table.

Ella pointed to plates. "Galaxy cupcakes!" With all the noise, I couldn't actually hear her say it. But I watched the way her mouth moved. And the cupcakes had purple-and-blue swirled frosting. So it wasn't hard to figure out.

"They're so pretty!" I looked to where Lana stood against the wall. She looked tired. I passed a cupcake to her, and she nodded in thanks.

Sinking my teeth into my own, I closed my eyes. They tasted just as good as they looked!

At the front, Ms. Ruiz clapped her hands. "Great job today, everyone! Now, we have a special treat, thanks to a friend of Lana's."

The lights dimmed. A video started on the TV at the front of the room. Ms. Ruiz put my clip-on mic in front of it.

In the video, a young woman waved. "Hello to Ms. Ruiz's Shooting Stars! I'm Emily. I'll be giving you a virtual tour of Space-E today!"

My eyes bugged. From the wall, Lana winked at me.

Ella squeezed my hand. Veejay and Dominic grinned.

I turned back to the screen. As Emily opened the doors into Space-E's rocket testing center, I gasped. It was a giant warehouse filled with real rocket parts!

It may not have been the same as going in person, but this was pretty great. I really *was* lucky.

AUTHOR'S NOTE

I'm an audiologist who supports access to language—whether it be spoken, signed, or both. I've written Astrid with hearing aids and spoken language because I'm the most familiar with that perspective, but I have great respect for the Deaf community and signed languages like American Sign Language (ASL). There are a lot of great books out there with deaf/hard-of-hearing characters that are written from other perspectives. For a starter list, find my profile on Instagram @rienealwriter.

ACKNOWLEDGMENTS

First of all, thank you to YOU, Astrid's readers! I hope this book inspires you to reach for the stars.

As Astrid learns, things just don't work unless you find your team. I am very grateful to have the amazing Carrie Pestritto as my agent. It honestly would not have occurred to me to write an original chapter book series without her guidance. Thank you also to my wonderful editor, Alyson Heller, who saw exactly what I was trying to do with Astrid and loved her from the beginning—and to all the people at Aladdin and Simon & Schuster who made this book into a reality. I'm so honored to get to work with you all.

Many thanks to Danielle Kelsay, Diane Niebuhr, Stephanie Fleckenstein, and everyone else at the University of Iowa Au.D. program, for my education in audiology. Thank you to all the hospitals, clinics, schools, and other places that harbored me as an intern and to all the clients who inspired me along the way. (And special thanks to Amanda Baum, who helped a ton with drummer info for my last project and whom I wasn't able to thank properly then.)

I wouldn't have gotten this far without Leira K. Lewis, Victoria Kazarian, Rosanna Griffin, and Rebecca Cuadra George. Whispering Platypodes forever! Thank you also to SCBWI. And a million warm fuzzies to Teresa Richards, who brought me up to speed on publishing when I started writing and remains the best critique partner ever.

Finally, super big thanks to JMac and SL for putting up with their mom being sucked into pretend worlds all the time. Thank you to my parents for all their love and support. Thank you to Grammy & Pa, for all the visits to NASA Ames over the years. And thank you to Brian, who supported my writing from the beginning. I love you and would not be here without you. Finally, thank you to God for this opportunity.

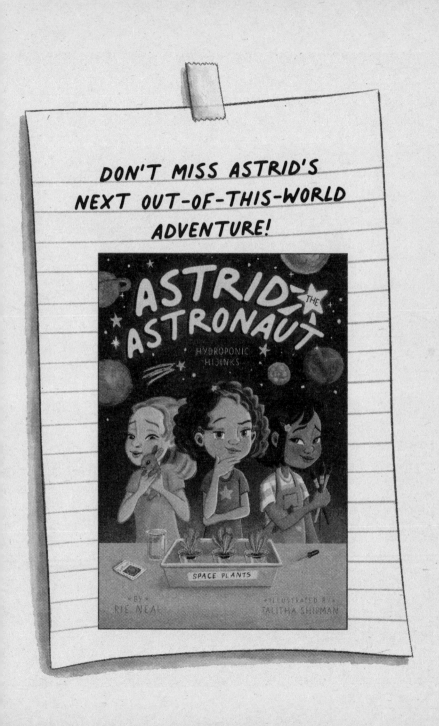

DON'T MISS ASTRID'S NEXT OUT-OF-THIS-WORLD ADVENTURE!

A GREAT TEAMMATE

"Over here!" I shouted. My feet flew through the grass. I slid a finger behind my hearing aids to get rid of the sweat there.

My best friend, Hallie, nodded. She slammed the soccer ball over to me.

A kid from the other team ran up, and I pivoted to block the ball. This shot was *mine*.

With short kicks, I dodged around him. But he wasn't giving up. He stuck a hand out to throw me off, but I twirled around it.

Veejay, my other best friend, ran up. Two kids from the other team were right behind him. "Astrid!" he panted. "Pearl is open!"

He was right. Pearl stood in front of the goal, waving her arms.

We'd been playing soccer every recess this week, and I was getting really good. But Pearl had just started playing with us yesterday. If I passed to her, I didn't know for sure if she'd score. I *knew* what *my* feet could do.

So I kept the ball close, making my way down the field.

Hallie ran up. She shouted something, but I didn't hear it.

I was close enough now. I could make the shot. So I pulled my right foot back and launched the ball at the goal.

Smack! The boy who'd been guarding me stomped his foot in to steal the ball, then passed it to a teammate.

"Get the ball!" Hallie shouted to Ella. But Ella wasn't fast enough. The other team slammed the ball into their goal just as the recess bell buzzed.

Pearl stomped over. She tossed her long blond ponytail over a shoulder. "Why didn't you pass me the ball?"

I shrugged. "I wanted to make sure we won."

"Ugh!" Pearl threw up her hands. "Well, we lost. You're the worst teammate ever, Astrid!"

As Pearl ran back across the blacktop,

Hallie caught up to me. "Veejay said he'd take the ball back." She frowned at me. "What's wrong?"

I was still staring after Pearl. I wasn't a bad teammate. I'd just wanted us to win. And that was a good thing, right?

My sweatshirt suddenly felt way too hot. I fluffed my ponytail over my neck to cool off.

"Can we stop for a sec?" I asked. At the edge of the field, I yanked my sweatshirt up over my head.

Pop went my right hearing aid, flying off my ear.

"Oh no!" I shouted.

"I see it!" Hallie said. "It's by the tree."

We stepped closer to look. And yep—a sparkly blue hearing aid sat in the dirt. I picked it up, wiping the earmold off on my shirt.

"Hey, look!" Hallie pointed. A tuft of soft brown fur wiggled into a hole near the roots of the tree.

"It's a baby bunny!" I gasped. Two tiny, furry noses poked out.

"A whole nest of them!" Hallie squealed.

The blacktop was mostly empty now. "We'd better go," I said, fitting the hearing aid back in my ear.

As we jogged back to class, Pearl's words sat like a lump of sticky oatmeal in my stomach. Astronauts were great at teamwork, and I was going to be an astronaut one day. So either I wasn't good enough, or Pearl was wrong. And I was *definitely* good enough. I had a long way to go, sure, but I worked hard in school. I was good at math. I was in Shooting Stars, our after-school, space-themed club. And I was going to find a way to go to Space Camp this summer. Which meant Pearl was wrong. Anyway, I'd wanted us to win, so I was a *great* teammate. Pearl was the problem.

At least I didn't have to work with her in Shooting Stars.